Tallulah and the Tea Leaves

Tallulah and the Tea Leaves

by Louise John
and Vian Oelofsen

Evans

For my Amelia - LJ

First published 2008
Evans Brothers Limited
2A Portman Mansions
Chiltern St
London W1U 6NR

British Library Cataloguing in Publication Data

John, Louise
    Tallulah and the tea leaves. - (Skylarks)
    1. Children's stories
    I. Title
    823.9'2[J]

ISBN: 978 0 237 53584 1 (HB)
ISBN: 978 0 237 53596 4 (PB)

Printed in China by WKT Co. Ltd

Series Editor: Louise John
Design: Robert Walster
Production: Jenny Mulvanny

Contents

Chapter One

"Muuum," whinged Tallulah for the hundredth time that day, "I'm bored, bored, BORED!"

"Yes, Tallulah, I know," sighed Mum patiently. "Why don't you read a book? Or play outside in the garden?"

"Don't want to," said Tallulah sulkily,

throwing herself face down on the sofa.

"Suit yourself, then," said Mum.

It was the summer holidays and the days drifted by endlessly. They'd been to

the beach and she'd been to tea at Sophie's house, but Tallulah had never been more bored in her life.

Suddenly the phone rang, making Tallulah jump.

"Yes… right… hmm," she heard Mum say. Then, "That'll be lovely. Tallulah will be pleased."

Tallulah sat up with interest. Maybe it was an invite to Emily's party? About time too! It would be unbearable if she were the only person in the class not to be invited.

"Guess what, Tallulah?" Mum asked, smiling. "I've got some news that'll cheer you up. Great-granny's coming to stay!"

Tallulah's heart sank. This wasn't good news. This wasn't even bad news.

It was really, really terrible news! Tallulah didn't like Great-granny very much. Not very much at all, really.

"She looks a bit like a witch," Tallulah once giggled to Sophie. "She's got funny straggly hair and a huge crooked nose!"

On the other hand, Great-granny was more than a bit fond of Tallulah. "Come here and give your old great-granny a cuddle," she'd say every time she arrived, and Tallulah would brace herself. She wrinkled up her nose and shuddered at the mere thought of it.

"She's coming later tonight," said Mum. "Don't worry, though, Tallulah, you can see her first thing in the morning for breakfast."

"Fantastic," muttered Tallulah through gritted teeth. "Just fantastic."

Chapter Two

"Good morning, Tallulah, dear," smiled Great-granny, slurping a cup of tea. "Come here and give your old great-granny a cuddle."

Dad smirked behind his newspaper. "Right, I'm off to work!" he said. "See you later."

A bit of tea missed Great-granny's
mouth and trickled slowly down her
chin. Tallulah sighed. She really
was disgusting.

"Is there any toast, please, Mum?" she
asked, slumping at the table.

"Having a good holiday, Tallulah?"
asked Great-granny.

"Bored, bored, bored, bored," mumbled Tallulah.

"Well, we'll see what we can do about that," said Great-granny and gave Tallulah a wink. "Let's read the tea leaves and see what they've got to say about Tallulah today."

Great-granny swilled the dregs of her tea around in the bottom of her cup and took a last gulp. Mum grinned.

"Some people say that you can tell the future by looking at the bits of tea left in the bottom of your teacup," explained Great-granny. "They make a picture. It's a real skill. Passed down from generation to generation. My own grandmother taught me."

Tallulah snorted. Great-granny peered down into the bottom of the cup.

"I can see here, Tallulah, that things
are about to change. Now, what's this I
can see? It looks like a mermaid.
Hmm, yes, it's definitely a mermaid.
How very peculiar."

"Come on, Tallulah," smiled Mum. "Upstairs to get washed and dressed, please. We're off to visit the new aquarium in town today."

Tallulah raced upstairs. Something fun to do at last, even if it was with Great-granny!

Chapter Three

The new aquarium had only been open
for a few weeks and there were crowds
of people everywhere Tallulah looked.

"I'm off to see the stingrays," she
shouted to Great-granny and Mum,
racing ahead.

As Tallulah stood with her nose

pressed up against the enormous tank,
she caught a glimpse of something
sparkling in a far corner. She screwed up
her eyes and looked a bit closer. It didn't
look much like a stingray. It looked more
like a large shimmering fish tail. In fact,
it looked just like a mermaid.

"No," whispered Tallulah to herself quietly, "I'm imagining it. Mermaids belong in storybooks."

She looked again, and sure enough, a beautiful mermaid appeared in front of her. The mermaid smiled at Tallulah and beckoned with her hand. Tallulah frowned. Step through a window made of solid glass? Impossible.

Nevertheless, as Tallulah stepped forward she heard a loud whooshing noise and was suddenly surrounded by water. She was swimming underwater!

In the distance, through the thick glass of the tank, Tallulah could just about make out Mum and Great-granny chatting together. It was as if they couldn't see her. The mermaid beckoned again. Looking down in bewilderment at

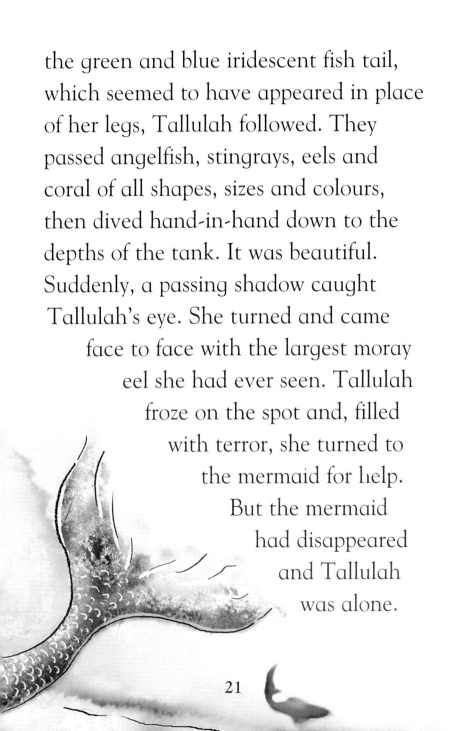

the green and blue iridescent fish tail,
which seemed to have appeared in place
of her legs, Tallulah followed. They
passed angelfish, stingrays, eels and
coral of all shapes, sizes and colours,
then dived hand-in-hand down to the
depths of the tank. It was beautiful.
Suddenly, a passing shadow caught
Tallulah's eye. She turned and came
    face to face with the largest moray
    eel she had ever seen. Tallulah
    froze on the spot and, filled
    with terror, she turned to
    the mermaid for help.
    But the mermaid
    had disappeared
    and Tallulah
    was alone.

With a flick of its tail, the eel advanced with gaping jaws. At the very last second, a hand reached for Tallulah and pulled her to safety behind a rock. Tallulah began to gasp. She needed air and quickly. She flipped her tail and headed to the surface of the pool. There was another loud whoosh and she found herself standing exactly where she'd started – on the outside of the tank, fully-clothed.

"Mum, Great-granny!" she yelled. "Did you see that? Did you see what just happened?"

"See what, dear?" asked Great-granny with a twinkle in her eye.

Chapter Four

"Tallulah!" shouted Mum. "Time to get up. I'm not going to call you again!"

"Okay, okay, I'm coming," she mumbled. Tallulah had hardly slept a wink. Weird and wonderful dreams of mermaids, sea creatures and moray eels had left her feeling shattered.

"You look tired, poppet," smiled Mum.
Everything okay?"

"Hmmph," said Tallulah.

"Tallulah," said Dad in his 'you're in
trouble' voice, "you know, I really
wanted to have a little chat with you
this morning. All that nonsense

yesterday about mermaids and swimming underwater. You should know better, Tallulah. It's one thing having a vivid imagination, and quite another to…"

"Morning!" boomed Great-granny, bustling into the kitchen.

"How's Tallulah?" she asked, grinning. "Ready for another boring day?"

After breakfast, Great-granny swished the dregs of her tea around in the bottom of her cup and then drained it.

"Right, let's have a look what we have here. Goodness, what's this I can see... I wonder what that means…"

"Great-granny!" shouted an impatient Tallulah. "What is it?"

"Well, dear, it looks like a space rocket. Shooting off."

"Rockets don't 'shoot off', Great-granny. They blast off into outer space to explore planets."

"Yes, dear, that's what I'm worried about," mumbled Great-granny.

"Come on, you two," grumbled Mum. "Or we'll never get out. We're off to the Science Museum today."

Chapter Five

The Science Museum wasn't really up Tallulah's street at all. The highlight of the day so far had been a fizzy ice-cream soda in the teashop. Delicious!

"Come on," said Mum. "We'll just have a quick look at the space section and then we'll head home."

"At last," muttered Tallulah. "What a dull place!"

As much as Tallulah hated to admit it, the space section did look interesting. Models of rockets and lunar landers were displayed all around, not to mention a space suit that had been worn by a real astronaut.

Ignoring the 'Do Not Touch' sign, Tallulah picked up the helmet.

"Hurry!" she suddenly heard a man's voice yell. "You'd better get that on. We've got a planet to save!"

Tallulah looked up in alarm. Great-granny and Mum were looking intently at a display about Mars and didn't seem to have heard anything at all.

Quickly, Tallulah put on the helmet. She opened her eyes, peeped through the visor and found herself sitting in the command module of a rocket!

"Permission to launch?" shouted a loud voice.

"Counting down," shouted another. "10, 9, 8, 7, 6, 5, 4, 3, 2, 1…Blast off!"

The rocket zoomed into space, taking Tallulah with it. She held her breath as they soared past planets and stars.

After some time, the rocket landed on a glowing yellow planet. Tallulah stepped out of the hatch and was instantly swept off her feet. She bounced and floated weightlessly. But when she turned around, the crew had disappeared.

In the distance, she could hear the sound

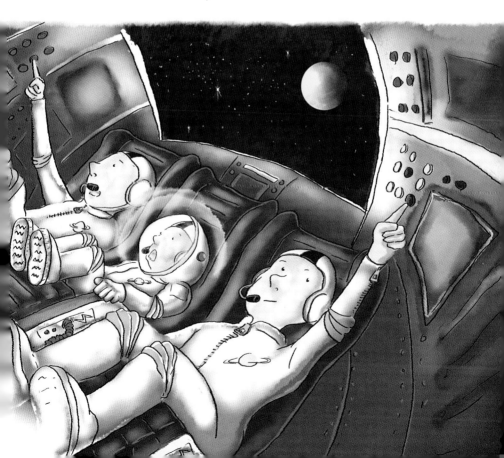

of fighting and space zappers. Aliens!
What was she doing here wasting time,
when she had work to do? Tallulah set
off to join the fight but immediately
came face to face with the oddest-
looking creature she had ever seen. It
gurgled and screeched and reached out
a green tentacle. Tallulah started to
panic. She reached for her space zapper,
but it was nowhere to be found. The

alien came closer and closer and Tallulah closed her eyes. This was surely the end.

Suddenly, and with no warning, the alien exploded into a mass of sticky green slime and gloop. The crew had returned, and zapped the alien just in time! Tallulah wiped the gunk from her visor with a trembling hand. Talk about a close shave!

"Well done, men!" the commander shouted as the crew floated back to the rocket. Then there was a sudden flash of light and, blinking and squinting, Tallulah found herself right back where she had started – in the museum!

"Hey, Tallulah, look at these funny gravity boots!" said Great-granny, grinning. "I bet you've never seen anything like this before?"

Chapter Six

Tallulah woke with a start after yet another troubled night. She wandered downstairs.

"Morning, Mum," she said. "I've been thinking. Wouldn't it be nice if we just stayed at home today?"

"Well, I thought we might go to…"

started Mum as Great-granny breezed into the kitchen.

"Ooh, eggs!" she cried. "Lovely. Sunny-side up for me, please."

"Let's have a look at the tea leaves again, Tallulah," she continued. "Who knows what we'll see today?"

Tallulah groaned as Great-granny swirled the remains of Mum's cold tea around in the bottom of the cup and flung it into the spider plant!

"Hmm. Looks like a trunk!" she muttered, peering into the cup.

Despite herself, Tallulah leaned over to look.

"Ooh, a holiday maybe?" she breathed.

"No, not that sort of trunk, dear," laughed Great-granny. "An elephant's trunk, of course."

Well, that all sounded fairly harmless, thought Tallulah. Elephants were quite sweet, now she came to think of it.

"So, Mum. What were you about to say earlier? Where are we going today?"

"Oh, yes, erm, the zoo. I've got us some tickets for the zoo," smiled Mum.

Chapter Seven

"I love the zoo!" cried Tallulah. "What shall we look at first?"

"Let's go and see the penguins. It's feeding time at 10 o'clock," said Mum.

After the penguins, they strolled through the zoo gardens, past the lions until they came to the elephant enclosure. An elephant plodded slowly over and tickled Tallulah gently with its trunk. The crowd laughed. Tallulah patted it. Yes, harmless, she smiled to herself.

Then the wind rushed past Tallulah's ears. Suddenly, she found herself travelling at great speed over bumpy ground in what seemed to be a jeep.

"Arrrgggh!" she screamed.

"Hang on!" a voice shouted. "They're gaining on us!"

Tallulah turned in the direction of the voice. A young man wearing safari clothing was driving the jeep at what felt like about a hundred miles an hour.

"Who are?" shouted Tallulah in alarm, gripping the sides of the jeep for dear life.

The man looked at Tallulah like she was crazy. "The elephants, of course!" he yelled.

Tallulah glanced over her shoulder and desperately wished she hadn't. Elephants. An elephant stampede, in fact! Hundreds of furious elephants were chasing after them at breakneck speed.

The elephants gained more and more ground. They grew closer and closer. Any closer and she would be able to touch them! Their stampeding feet churned up the dirt of the hot African plain and Tallulah could taste the dust in her throat.

Suddenly, she spotted a narrow opening in the bush ahead. "Look over there!" she shouted, pointing to the hidden track. "Head for the trees!"

"I'll never get this jeep through there!' yelled the driver.

"TRY! Or we're dead meat!"

At the very last minute the jeep
swerved off to the right and veered
down the track. It was just a few metres
across. After a moment, the driver

applied the brakes and the jeep screeched to a sudden halt, dragging branches and trees with it. The elephants carried on stampeding past Tallulah and past the hidden jeep.

Tallulah closed her eyes and tried to breathe normally. If it was excitement and adventure she'd been looking for this holiday, you certainly couldn't beat an elephant stampede for that.

Suddenly the wind whistled in her ears again, and she found herself standing back in the zoo being nuzzled by the same elephant as earlier on.

"Run! Elephants!" she shouted at the top of her voice.

"Tallulah? What on earth...?" cried Mum, as the crowd looked on in astonishment.

Chapter Eight

"Time to look at the tea leaves, Tallulah," said Great-granny the next morning.

"Wait, Great-granny, no," said Tallulah quickly, remembering the elephant experience with a shudder.

"Today I think I'd just like to be

Tallulah. Go to the park, play with my friends, you know, the usual boring stuff."

"Yes," said Great-granny grinning, "I hoped that might be the case, dear."

And, chuckling, she picked up her bag and made her way to the door to leave.

"I'm off home. See you soon," she smiled. "Enjoy the rest of the holidays!"

If you enjoyed this story, why not read another *Skylarks* book?

Ghost Mouse

by Karen Wallace and Beccy Blake

When the new owners of Honeycomb Cottage move in, the mice that live there are not happy. They like the cottage just as it is and Melanie and Hugo have plans to change everything. But the mice of Honeycomb Cottage are no ordinary mice. They set out to scare Melanie and Hugo away. They *are* ghost mice after all, and isn't that what ghosts do best?

Yasmin's Parcels
by Jill Atkins and Lauren Tobia

Yasmin lives in a tiny house with her mama and papa and six little brothers and sisters. They are poor and hungry and, as the oldest child, Yasmin knows she needs to do something to help. So, she sets off to find some food. But Yasmin can't find any food and, instead, is given some mysterious parcels. How can these parcels help her feed her family?

Skylarks titles include:

Awkward Annie
by Julia Williams and Tim Archbold
HB 9780237533847
PB 9780237534028

Sleeping Beauty
by Louise John and Natascia Ugliano
HB 9780237533861
PB 9780237534042

Detective Derek
by Karen Wallace and Beccy Blake
HB 9780237533885
PB 9780237534066

Hurricane Season
by David Orme and Doreen Lang
HB 9780237533892
PB 9780237534073

Spiggy Red
by Penny Dolan and Cinzia Battistel
HB 9780237533854
PB 9780237534035

London's Burning
by Pauline Francis and Alessandro
Baldanzi
HB 9780237533878
PB 9780237534059

The Black Knight
by Mick Gowar and Graham Howells
HB 9780237535803
PB 9780237535926

Ghost Mouse
by Karen Wallace and Beccy Blake
HB 9780237535827
PB 9780237535940

Yasmin's Parcels
by Jill Atkins and Lauren Tobia
HB 9780237535858
PB 9780237535971

Muffin
by Anne Rooney and Sean Julian
HB 9780237535810
PB 9780237535933

Tallulah and the Tea Leaves
by Louise John and Vian Oelofsen
HB 9780237535841
PB 9780237535964

The Big Purple Wonderbook
by Enid Richemont and Kelly Waldek
HB 9780237535834
PB 9780237535957